KONDO & KEZUMI
ARE NOT ALONE

Written by David Goodner
Illustrated by Andrea Tsurumi

Ⓛ Ⓑ
LITTLE, BROWN AND COMPANY
New York Boston

1

A Tiny Detour

Kondo and Kezumi lived on an island with crooked old trees and a crooked old tower, with fluffle-bunnies and flitter-birds, and with plenty of sparkleberries and all the comforts of home. Because it *was* home. Only they hadn't been there for a long time.

Kondo and Kezumi had been following a map.

They had visited new places.

They had met new friends.

They had tried new things.

And now it was time to go home.

Of course, they didn't go STRAIGHT home.

For one thing, they had to sail around a big storm.

Big storms were no fun to sail through.

Plus, they wanted to visit a few more islands.

"Do you think we can get to Improbable Island?" Kondo asked.

"Unlikely," said Kezumi. "But Doughnut Island looks interesting."

"It does," Kondo agreed. "I hope we get there before breakfast."

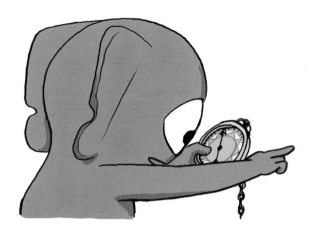

Kezumi traced a line on the map with her finger. Then she studied her compass. Finally, she pointed out to sea. "We need to go that way, toward Tiny Island. We'll catch the best wind to get us home."

"Dairy Isle is nearby, too," Kondo said. "That's one of my favorite places. At least before noon."

Kezumi turned the rudder. Kondo adjusted the mast. And together they set sail for home. Generally.

Luckily, they reached Doughnut Island before breakfast.

"There are no doughnuts," Kondo said, disappointed. "Not even glazed ones."

"Well, it is very round." Kezumi tried to cheer Kondo up. "And those pretty rocks look like sprinkles."

Even with sprinkles, the pretty rocks did not taste very good.

Kondo and Kezumi were still hungry
for adventure when they left Doughnut Island.
They were glad to see another speck on the
horizon.

"Is that Tiny Island?" Kondo asked. "It looks
too big to be tiny."

They sailed closer.

The island didn't get any smaller, but it did get
more beautiful.

Kondo's and Kezumi's hopes
grew bigger. It was time
for a tiny detour.

II

A Big Hello

They landed on a not-so-tiny beach. Kezumi jumped off the boat and nearly stepped on something small. That kind of thing usually happened to Kondo.

"Whoops!" Kezumi laughed. "I didn't see you!"

Kondo leaped out of the boat after Kezumi. He looked at Kezumi's feet and gasped. "It's a Teeny," he said. Kondo waved his biggest wave. "HELLO, TEENY!"

"A Teeny?" said Kezumi. "What's a Teeny?"

"That!" Kondo pointed at the little creature. "HELLO, TEENY!" he yelled again.

"I can see it, Kondo," said Kezumi. "But what IS it?"

Kondo pulled out the
map. "I'll show you."

He turned the map
this way…

and that way…

and the other way…

until finally he found
what he was looking for.

tiny Island

Teeny

"Look!" said Kondo. "There's a picture of a Teeny! Right here on Tiny Island."

Kondo and Kezumi hunched over the map for a closer look at the picture. It wasn't very big.

Then they knelt down in the sand for a closer look at the Teeny. The Teeny was smaller than the picture.

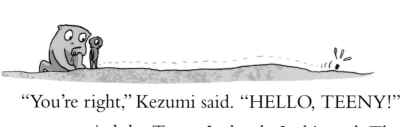

"You're right," Kezumi said. "HELLO, TEENY!"

"Eek!" cried the Teeny. It shook. It shivered. Then the Teeny ran away as fast as it could (which wasn't very fast).

"I think we scared it," said Kezumi.

"I think you're right," said Kondo.

Kondo and Kezumi watched the Teeny scurry up the beach and hide in a heap of seashells and seaweed and sea gunk.

"We should say *sorry*," said Kondo.

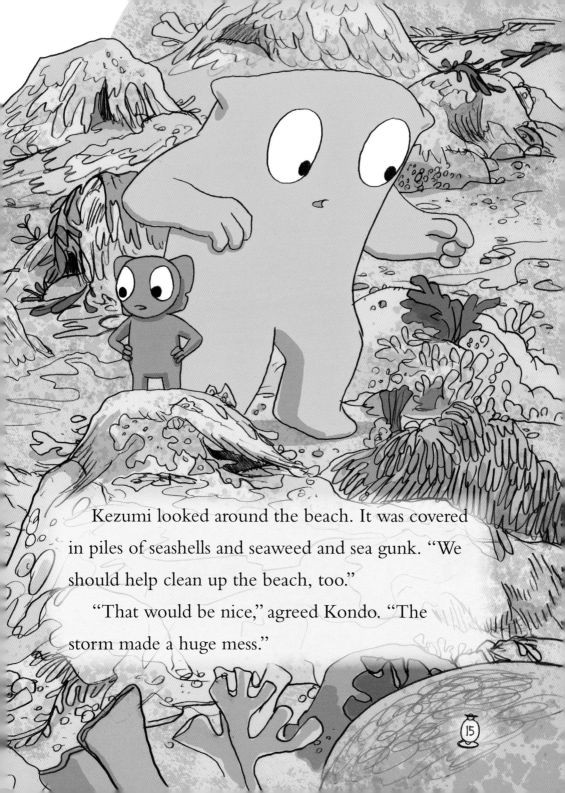

Kezumi looked around the beach. It was covered in piles of seashells and seaweed and sea gunk. "We should help clean up the beach, too."

"That would be nice," agreed Kondo. "The storm made a huge mess."

III

A Teeny Mistake

Kondo and Kezumi walked as quietly as they could over to the Teeny's hiding spot. Very carefully, Kezumi tossed away the seashells. Very gently, Kondo pulled off the clumps of seaweed and the globs of sea gunk.

They kept tossing and pulling until the entire pile was gone and all that was left was…

...one terrified Teeny.

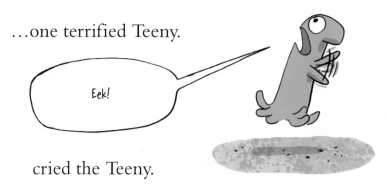

Eek!

cried the Teeny.

"SHHH!" shushed Kezumi.

"It's okay," said Kondo. "We're friends."

"Eek!" the Teeny cried again. It ran away as fast as it could (which still wasn't very fast) to the nearest mound of muck.

"It's definitely afraid of us," said Kezumi.

"Maybe if we keep cleaning, the Teeny will see we're trying to help," said Kondo.

Kezumi carefully tossed more seashells. Kondo gently pulled more clumps of seaweed and more globs of sea gunk. They tossed and pulled until all that was left were…

…TWO terrified Teenies.

"*Eek!*" the Teenies screeched.

"We're sorry!" Kezumi pleaded.

"Don't be scared," Kondo cried.

Telling someone not to be scared hardly ever works. The two Teenies took off as fast as they could to the next heap of seashells and seaweed and sea gunk.

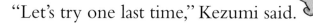

"Let's try one last time," Kezumi said.

"Okay," Kondo said. "But we need to be super, extra careful not to scare them."

Kondo and Kezumi tiptoed over to the Teenies' new hidey-hole. This time, Kondo silently picked up the entire mess at once and Kezumi delicately scooped up all that was left…

…THREE terrified Teenies!

"Eeeek!!!" the Teenies screeched.

Kondo and Kezumi tried to smile nicely at them.

"EEEEK!" the Teenies screamed louder.

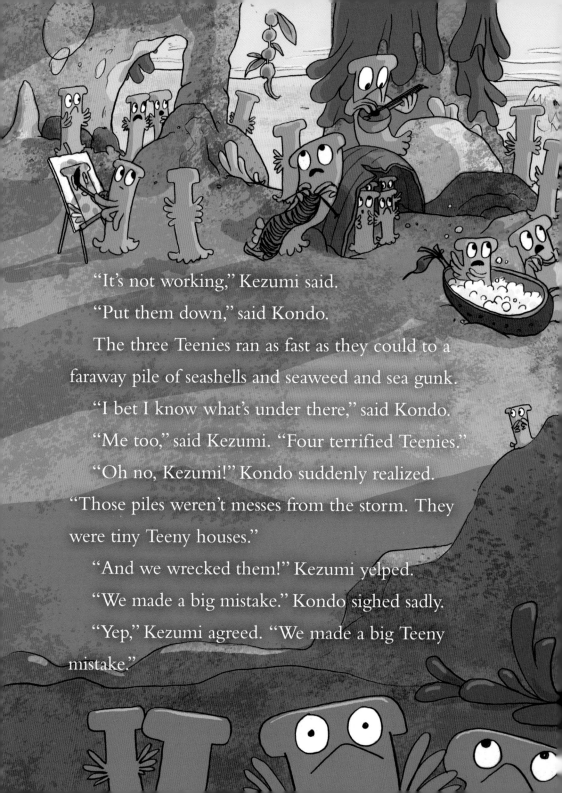

"It's not working," Kezumi said.

"Put them down," said Kondo.

The three Teenies ran as fast as they could to a faraway pile of seashells and seaweed and sea gunk.

"I bet I know what's under there," said Kondo.

"Me too," said Kezumi. "Four terrified Teenies."

"Oh no, Kezumi!" Kondo suddenly realized. "Those piles weren't messes from the storm. They were tiny Teeny houses."

"And we wrecked them!" Kezumi yelped.

"We made a big mistake." Kondo sighed sadly.

"Yep," Kezumi agreed. "We made a big Teeny mistake."

IV
Land Hooome!

Fixing a mess is usually harder than making one. It took Kondo and Kezumi a long time to gather up all the seashells and seaweed, and to glue it all back together with sea gunk.

After a while, the Teenies came out to help, too.
Once they finished, Kondo and Kezumi left
Tiny Island without making a peep.

"Goodbye!" Kezumi waved from the boat.

"Good luck!" Kondo whisper-yelled.

Three Teenies crept out to the shore. "EEEEK!!!" they yelled and raced back to their new Tiny Island homes.

The rough water quickly whisked Kondo and
Kezumi away. They didn't sail straight home, though.
Kondo wanted to stay far away from Spooky Island.

And they just HAD to swing by the Dairy Isle.

Finally…

"I see it!" Kezumi cheered. "Land *hoo*ome!"

Kondo rowed harder. "I can't wait!"

"If we'd skipped the Dairy Isle," Kezumi said, "we'd be home already."

"Home without any cheese!" Kondo said. He patted the two buckets of cheese they'd collected.

"Does our island look different to you?" Kezumi asked.

Kondo squinted. "Maybe? We've been gone a long time."

They sailed in
on the evening tide,
with the sun at their backs.
The wind carried them toward their
special cove, where they had found the
map and where they had built
their first boat.

Only…there was already a boat there. And it looked very familiar.

"Is that our boat?" Kondo asked.

"That *is* our boat," Kezumi declared. "How did it get here?"

"Maybe it drifted back."

"I doubt it," Kezumi said. "Without someone to steer, it could have gone anywhere. Or nowhere! Or sunk! Or crashed!"

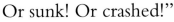

Kezumi hopped out of their new boat and ran over to their old boat. "Look!" she said. "The sail turned into a roof."

"That would have been nice on hot days," Kondo mused.

"I'll put a roof on our next boat," Kezumi promised. "Not over the whole boat, though. I like to see the stars."

"We're not building a new boat right away, are we?" Kondo asked.

"No," Kezumi said. "But we should tie up this boat. Then I'm going to bed. I miss my bed."

"Me too," Kondo agreed. "We're not building a new boat tomorrow either, are we?"

Kezumi laughed. "No, Kondo. We're staying home. Nothing could make us leave right now."

V

Something Makes Them Leave

Kondo and Kezumi gathered their stuff and trooped up to the crooked old tower.

"Does it look different to you?" Kezumi asked.

"Maybe it's just dark," Kondo said.

It *was* dark, after all. The sun was almost down, and the lamps Kondo and Kezumi usually kept lit had gone out a long time ago. But Kezumi was pretty sure the tower looked different.

Kondo took the stairs two at a
time. Kezumi tried to keep up.

"There are leaves everywhere,"
she said, moving a vine out of
the way.

"We haven't been
here to clean,"
Kondo explained.

He got to the
door, which was
covered in long
palm fronds. "Ugh.
Help me pull these
down."

With some work, they got the door uncovered.
Kondo opened it.

KREEEEEK!

"We need to oil that," he said.

The inside of the house was

dark. Kondo stepped inside.

SQUELCH

"Ewww," he said. "Did the roof leak?" But the leak didn't smell like water. Or feel like water. It felt like jelly. Cold jelly.

And there was a smell. Not a bad smell. It was a sharp citrusy smell that stuck at the back of the throat and tickled the top of the nose.

"Kezumi, I think something is wrong with the tower."

Kezumi did not say *Oh really?* and roll her eyes like she wanted to. Instead, she said, "Light the lantern."

They kept a lamp by the door,
and they'd made sure to fill it up
before they left.

Flickering light filled the room, casting deep shadows.
A shimmery trail wound all through the tower.

"SLIME!" Kondo and Kezumi yelled.

Kezumi checked the shelves. "There's slime on our
books!"

Kondo checked the cupboards. "There's
slime on our food!"

The trail of goo led into the dark…toward their bedroom.

"We should go down there," Kezumi said. She didn't go down there.

Kondo also didn't go down there. "We should."

Kondo edged forward. Kezumi scooted closer. Kondo leaned over the railing.

The lamplight shined down.

BURBLE!

Something burbled.

"Stay back!" Kondo staggered away from the noise.

Kezumi bravely held up the lamp for a closer look.

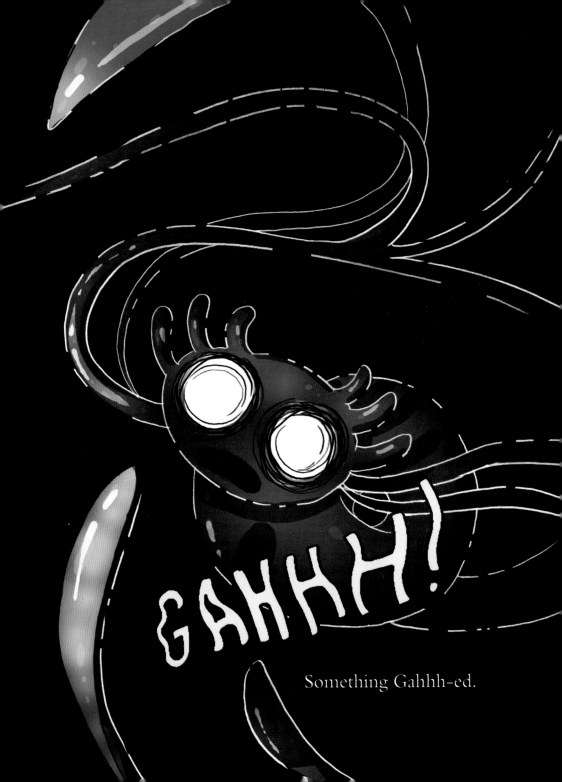

"AHHH!!!" Kondo and Kezumi yelled.

Two long, snaky arms waved up in the air at them.

"Run!" Kezumi hollered.

Kondo was way ahead of her. He took the stairs
two at a time and raced out of the tower. Kezumi
had no trouble keeping up.

VI

Unwelcome Home

They ran all the way back to the beach, past trees that looked like monster arms, through the bushes that smelled like monster breath, and over the wet rocks that felt like monster goo.

"What was that?" Kezumi asked when they finally stopped running.

"Whatever it was, it was spooky!" Kondo said. "Did we land on Spooky Island by mistake?"

"That doesn't seem very likely," Kezumi said.
"We passed Spooky Island a long time ago. I might
get us a little lost sometimes, but not *that* lost."

"What should we do?" Kondo wondered.

Kezumi had no idea. But she didn't want to admit it. "We should build a fire," she said at last. "To keep a lookout."

"Then we need a really big fire," Kondo said. He eyed the boat.

"No," Kezumi said.

"Driftwood?" Kondo asked.

Kezumi nodded yes.

Gathering wood from the beach was a cold, wet job. Instead of sleeping in their warm comfy beds, Kondo and Kezumi camped on the itchy sandy beach.

At least they had cheese for dinner.

While they toasted cubes of cheddar, Kezumi kept gazing up at the tower.

Kondo stared into the fire. "I know what we're doing in the morning," he said. "We're going back to our tower."

"Kondo." Kezumi sniffed. "I'm not sure it's our tower anymore."

VII

Kondo and Kezumi Return (Again)

Morning came. Kezumi hadn't slept well. She was tired. Kondo also hadn't slept well. He was cranky.

Kondo glared up at the tower. "Are you ready?"

Kezumi yawned and stretched and crackled. "To do what?"

"To take our home back," Kondo said. He wasn't quite sure how, but he was in no mood to let that stop him.

He stormed toward the tower with Kezumi following in his wake.

"Kondo, don't forget the lamp!" she said.

In the daytime, the tower looked terrible. The windows were smeared with mud. The sides were covered in leaves and bark. Sticks and stones were stuffed into every open crack.

"What a disaster!" Kondo exclaimed. He went from cranky to furious.

Kezumi was upset, too. "What a mess!"

They started to fix the disastrous mess.

Kondo ripped off the leaves and tore out the
sticks and stones. Kezumi scrubbed away the mud.
It took a long time, but eventually the tower began
to look more like their tower.

Kezumi peered through a window. "The other side is blocked, too."

Kondo tried the door. It was now locked. He shook it. He pounded on it.

It stayed locked.

"Don't break it, Kondo," Kezumi said. "Wait a minute." She went to a window and wiggled the latch free. The window didn't open very far, but Kezumi wasn't very big.

She shimmied and squeezed. She sucked in her tummy as much as she could.

Then she was through.

"Are you okay?" Kondo called out.

Kezumi didn't say anything.

Kondo waited.

"Kezumi!" he hissed.

Kondo worried. Anything could happen to Kezumi in there.

There was a noise inside. Was it the monster? Was the monster eating Kezumi RIGHT NOW? Kondo got ready to batter the door down.

The door opened.

"AHHH!" Kondo squealed and almost fell off the stairs.

VIII
Monster Things

K ezumi stood in the doorway. "Shhh," she said. "I think it's asleep."

"Shhh?" Kondo replied. "I don't want it to be asleep. I want it to be gone." He opened a gooey cabinet and pulled out another lamp, a bigger one. He gave the little one to Kezumi. "Here. Take this."

They crept through the house. Light poured
through the doorway, the open window, and from
the lamps. The rest of the house was dim and dusky.
Kondo stormed toward the bedroom stairs.
"Hey!" he called out. "We're not afraid of you."

In fact, he *was* kind of afraid. But now he was more angry than afraid. It felt better to be mad than to be scared.

Kondo shined the light down the stairs. "You have to leave!" Kondo dropped the light lower.

What he saw was…kind of cute.

Kezumi peeked over the railing. "Aww!
Kondo, it looks so sweet."

Kondo was not
convinced. "It might
be a monster."

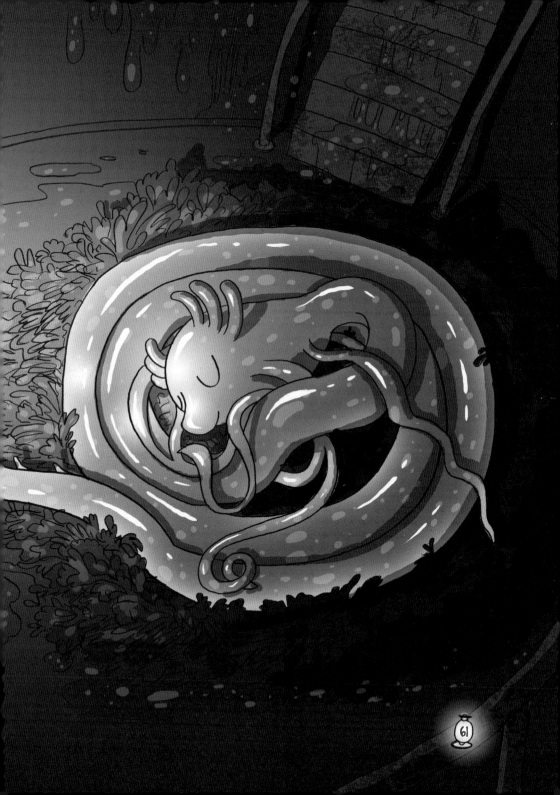

"How do you know if it's a monster?" Kezumi asked.

"It does monster things," Kondo said.

Kezumi scratched her head. "Like what?"

"Like stomp all over our island," Kondo said. "And ruin our house. And…and…scare us away!"

"Like what we did to the Teenies?"

Kondo was flustered. "That was different! We didn't mean to do all those things."

"But we did do them," Kezumi said.

"WE'RE NOT MONSTERS!" Kondo yelled.

"Are you sure?" Kezumi asked.

"Yes, I'm sure!" Kondo replied.

"Well then," said Kezumi, "maybe this isn't a monster, either."

"And maybe it is," Kondo huffed.

IX
What Is a Monster?

The maybe-a-monster was quiet.

Kondo and Kezumi thought about what to do next. Finally, Kondo had an idea.

"Let's try to say hello," he said. "But keep your light handy."

Kondo and Kezumi carefully climbed down the stairs. The maybe-a-monster still didn't move.

Kondo turned up the flame on his light. The room went bright.

The maybe-a-monster let out a monstrous cry.

Kondo and Kezumi let out their own monstrous cries.

AHHH!

The maybe-a-monster cried again.

BURBLE!

So did Kondo and Kezumi.

AHHH!

The *burbles* and *ahhhs* went back and forth
until everyone was *burbled* and *ahhhed* out.

Exhausted, Kezumi took a brave step forward.
The maybe-a-monster flinched away from her
lamp.

"Kondo," Kezumi said. "I think it's afraid of the light."

"What kind of a monster is afraid of the light?" Kondo asked.

"Let's turn off our lamps," Kezumi said.

"Too scary," said Kondo.

"What kind of monster is afraid of the dark?" burbled the maybe-a-monster.

This was a good time for Kondo and Kezumi to yell "Ahhh!" But they didn't. They were too tired—and they were maybe a little less afraid of the maybe-a-monster. Because maybe it wasn't a monster after all.

"Are you a monster?" Kezumi asked.

"No. I'm Susan," said Susan. "Are you monsters?"

"No," said Kezumi. "I'm Kezumi."

"And I'm Kondo," said Kondo.

"Hello," said Susan.

X

A Puzzling Discovery

Kondo and Kezumi and Susan had a lot of questions for one another. But mainly, they wanted to know how they all ended up here, in the crooked old tower, together.

"I found a map," said
Susan.

"We did, too!" said Kondo.

"And we built a boat to go exploring," said
Kezumi.

"I found a boat," said Susan.

"We know!" said Kondo.

"I wanted to go to this island." Susan rolled out
her map. It had different islands than Kondo and
Kezumi's map.

Susan pointed to a nice-looking island at the torn
edge of the map. Someone had written "Home" on it.

"Home sounded like a nice place to visit," said Susan.

Kondo and Kezumi looked at Susan's map.
Then they looked at their own map. Then they
realized something important.

"Our maps fit together," said Kondo.

"Like a puzzle," said Kezumi.

Kondo and Kezumi and Susan pieced the two maps together. That's when they realized they were all exactly where they were meant to be.

Home.

XI
Change of Plans

K ondo and Kezumi had found another new friend. Except this time, the friend found them.

They built a hut under the biggest sparkleberry bush. The friends covered it in mud and leaves and bark and palm fronds. It was the darkest spot on the entire island. Susan loved it.

75

At dusk (when the sun went down), Kondo and Kezumi and Susan ate dinner at the cove. At dawn (before the sun came up), they had breakfast under the shade of the crooked old tower. It was not too bright for Susan…and not too dark for Kondo and Kezumi.

One night, Kezumi had an idea. "We should trade maps," she said. "And keep exploring!"

Kondo wasn't so sure.

Neither was Susan.

But Kezumi was very convincing.

The friends switched maps. It was exciting to look at all there was to see.

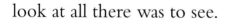

"There's something missing from this map,"
Kezumi said.

"You're right," Kondo agreed.

"I'll fix it."

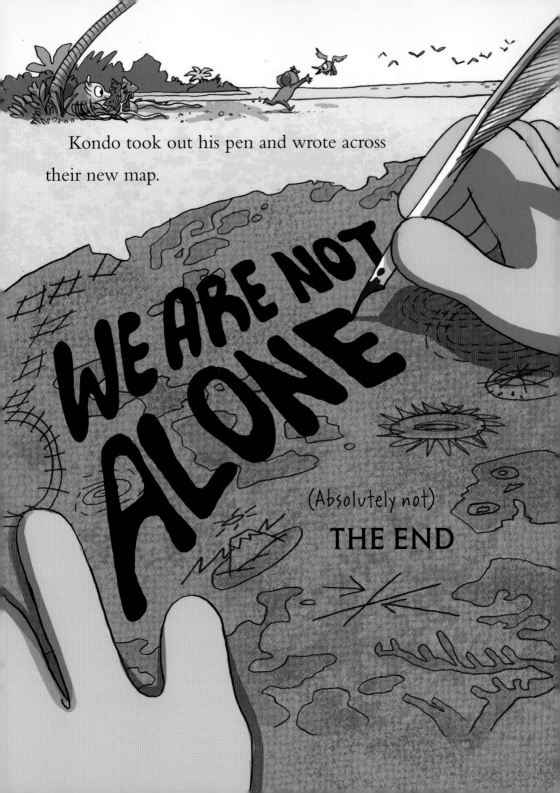

Kondo took out his pen and wrote across their new map.

WE ARE NOT ALONE

(Absolutely not)

THE END

EMBARK ON ALL THE
KONDO & KEZUMI ADVENTURES:

David Goodner lives in North Texas with his adoring wife, two tolerating cats, and one very enthusiastic dog. When he's not writing children's books, he works for the Arlington Public Library. He likes to make art, play role-playing games, and take naps.

Andrea Tsurumi is the author-illustrator of *Accident!* and *Crab Cake*, and the illustrator of *Not Your Nest*, *Sharko & Hippo*, and *Mr. Watson's Chickens*. Born and raised in New York, she now lives in Philadelphia with her spouse and their dog. When not inventing croissant-based animals, she likes reading about ordinary and ridiculous history and making comics. She invites you to visit her at andreatsurumi.com.

To Tracey Keevan.
We couldn't have made this voyage without you. —D.G.
For Molly Brooks and Maëlle Doliveux —A.T.

About This Book

The illustrations for this book were drawn in pencil and rendered digitally. This book was edited by Esther Cajahuaringa and designed by Jenny Kimura. The production was supervised by Virginia Lawther, and the production editor was Annie McDonnell. The text was set in Bembo MT Pro Regular, and the display type is Inagur Pro Regular.

Little, Brown and Company
Hachette Book Group
1290 Avenue of the Americas, New York, NY 10104
Visit us at LBYR.com

First Edition: April 2021

Little, Brown and Company is a division of Hachette Book Group, Inc.
The Little, Brown name and logo are trademarks of Hachette Book Group, Inc.

The publisher is not responsible for websites (or their content) that are not owned by the publisher.

Library of Congress Cataloging-in-Publication Data
Names: Goodner, David, author. | Tsurumi, Andrea, illustrator.
Title: Kondo & Kezumi are not alone / written by David Goodner ; illustrated by Andrea Tsurumi.
Other titles: Kondo and Kezumi are not alone
Description: First edition. | New York : Little, Brown and Company, 2021. | Series: Kondo & Kezumi ; [3]
| Audience: Ages 6-10. | Summary: When best friends Kondo and Kezumi return home from their island adventures they discover something unexpected occupying their tower.
Identifiers: LCCN 2020036515 | ISBN 9780759554726 (hardcover) | ISBN 9780759554719 (trade paperback)
Subjects: CYAC: Adventure and adventurers—Fiction. | Islands—Fiction. | Best friends—Fiction. | Friendship—Fiction. | Sea stories.
Classification: LCC PZ7.1.G6543 Ko 2021 | DDC [E]—dc23
LC record available at https://lccn.loc.gov/2020036515
ISBNs: 978-0-7595-5472-6 (hardcover), 978-0-7595-5471-9 (pbk.)

Printed in China

APS

Hardcover: 10 9 8 7 6 5 4 3 2 1
Paperback: 10 9 8 7 6 5 4 3 2 1